This story is for Pat.
We met when I was
seven and she has
been feeding me
chocolate brownies
ever since.
She is also a very
good friend.

PAT

LAUREN

a special thank you
to Emily who is
of course
the bee's knees

minal is a
bug

eggs
Milk
bread
celery
chocolate
Thank you
to the chic
caroline
valentine

Library of Congress
Cataloging-in-Publication
Data is available.
Library of Congress
Catalog Card Number
99-10713

First published
in Great Britain
in 1999 by
Orchard Books,
London
Designed by
Anna-Louise Billson

ISBN 0-7636-0961-7
2 4 6 8 10 9 7 5 3 1
Printed in Singapore
Candlewick Press
2067 Massachusetts Avenue
Cambridge,
Massachusetts 02140

This is me Clarice Bean

CANDLEWICK PRESS
CAMBRIDGE, MASSACHUSETTS

(I don't have
a watch so I've drawn
one on my arm in felt tip.)

I like peace and quiet but
I don't get much in my room.
I'm always busy rushing around.
My room is small so I have to
squash everything in.
I like to have lots of things
just in case.

I have this younger brother Minal Cricket.

We have to share so I have drawn a line down the middle.

If he puts one toe over my side he is sorry.

Minal Cricket likes to hang upside down until he turns a funny color. Then he sort of wriggles around like a maggot.

Sometimes I say, I haven't got time for all your nonsense.

And he says, Twit.

And I say,
Twit and a half.

And he says,
Twit with carrots
in your ears.

And then I flick his nose with my ruler,

And he says,
Mooom,

in this really whiny brother way.

And Mom says,
No flicking noses
with rulers.

And I say,
What do you flick
noses with then?

And she says,
Celery.

And I say,
We don't have any.

And she says,
No flicking noses then.

My sister Marcie has a room all to herself,
so she has peace and quiet whenever she wants.
Marcie likes to wear make-up and read about boys.
Whenever I have time on my hands I
peek around the door and try to make
her notice me.

She says,
Go away.
And I say,
Why?
**Because
I don't want to talk to you.**
Why?
**Because
you are very irritating.**
Why?
**Because
you are a little brat.**
Why?
**You better get
out of my room
before I count to ten.**

And I don't need to ask why.

???

do boys
give you the
dreamy eye?

Maarcie

My
older
brother
Kurt is usually
in his room with
his door shut.
He doesn't talk much
but he wears T-shirts
with writing on them.
They say,
SHUT UP AND GO AWAY.
Mom says,
He's at that difficult age.
Dad says,
He should try being
forty-four.
Mom says,
*It's not easy
being a teenager.*

Dad says,
It's no **picnic** being the father of one and it would **help** if he would stop grunting.

no entry nuclear waste

Mom says, *He's in the dark tunnel of adolescence.* But usually he's in his room.

Kurt says,
No one understands me.

happy about nothing

Shut up
Go away

bored beyond belief

Kurt says he wants to be left alone. Lucky for him he has a room all to himself that smells of socks.

I'm going **bananas** here, Bernard.

Dad has it made.
When he wants to be
left alone he goes to work.

He has a nice marbly office.
It's wall to wall windows
and office equipment.
He has a swiveling chair
and a desk the size of a bed.
It's full of important business
and you can only get to talk
to him if Ms. Egglington
buzzes you through.
When Dad wants some peace
and quiet Ms. Egglington says,

I'm afraid he's
in a meeting.

(i.e., buzz off.)
Really he's eating rocky road
ice cream and listening to
Frank Sinatra on the stereo.

I can't talk now,
I've got another
call coming through.

This thing's going
down faster than
a sinking soufflé.

you're dum dee dum dee dum dee dum Waldorf salad

Grandad spends all his time having peace and quiet. He is most often asleep in a chair with a cat on his head.

My brother Minal and I like to jump on him and snip his moustache with Mom's nail scissors.

Sometimes Grandad and I play cards.
Grandad's eyesight is on the blink
so normally I win.
He says,
Is that a Jack of Hearts?
And I say, No, it's a
Three of Spades,
Grandad.

Yesterday he poured a carton
of soup on his cornflakes.
He said,
I think this milk's **bad.**
It looks **a bit** lumpy.
I said, It's pea soup, Grandad.

When Mom wants some peace and quiet she balances on one leg in her bedroom or listens to whales singing in the tub.

Sometimes she has candles around the edges that smell. Other times she plays one of her "learn a foreign language in fourteen days" tapes.

She's learning Mandarin at the moment. So far she can say, I've spilt cobbler on my cardigan, and there's a spider hiding in my hotel room.

She likes speaking in other languages. It makes her feel like she is on vacation. Sometimes she'll say, Jeg er dødtræt af jer allesammen, which means "I've had it up to here with all of you" in Danish.

Sometimes I say, Mom do you ever get bored and she says, If only I had the time.

When I get a bee in my bonnet and Mom needs some
peace and quiet she says,

Go and run around in the yard.

This usually does the trick.

Sometimes I chuck potatoes over the neighbor's wall.

Because I might want to be an acrobat I have to keep nimble and flexible. I do this by scrunching into the laundry basket.

Getting out is the tricky part.

I do **balancing** and smiling in tights.

(That's a very important part of acrobatics.)

There's no peace and quiet in the yard
because there's this boy who lives next door.
He likes to call over the wall.
He says,

What are you **doing?**
Can I-I-I **play?**
I knooow you can **hear me.**

Grandad calls him Shouting Boy, but his name is Robert Granger. He always wants to know what I'm up to, and he always wants to do what I'm doing, which is normally twirling until I fall over.

Robert Granger doesn't have any ideas of his own — except copying me.

So I go indoors to do handstands quietly on my side of the room.

Then Minal starts playing football on my bed. He says he does it accidentally.

I say,

More like accidentally on purpose.

I get angry. So I "accidentally" chuck his blanket out the window. It lands on the dog next door and Dad gets in a fight with the neighbors.

Mother

Dad says,
Right now you are
not the flavor of
the month,
young lady.
Minal is grinning
like a smug twit
so I dump a bowl
of spaghetti on
his head.

I am in
big
trouble.

Mom says I should try to think before I act.
And she's right.
If I'd thought about it I would have put
    tapioca down his shorts.

I am in such **big** trouble that I get sent to **my room** for **3** whole hours. Alone.

I love it.

Finally, some peace and quiet.

The only time my family is quiet at the same time is when we sit down to watch our favorite show — Martians in the Kitchen.

The rest of the time it is non-stop noise but that's the way we (mostly) like it.

Uncle Ted (eating again)

Marcie (painting her nails)

kurt (smiling)

Dad

Yolla

Mom

Noah

Minal Cricket (not talking)